This book belongs to

_____

Characters (in order of appearance)

Narrator	DIEDRICH BADER
Elizabeth Swann	KEIRA KNIGHTLEY
Tai Huang	REGGIE LEE
Barbossa	GEOFFREY RUSH
Sao Feng	CHOW YUN-FAT
Will Turner	ORLANDO BLOOM
Pintel	LEE ARENBERG
Tia Dalma	NAOMIE HARRIS
Captain Jack Sparrow	JOHNNY DEPP
Lord Cutler Beckett	TOM HOLLANDER
"Bootstrap Bill" Turner	STELLAN SKARSGÅRD
Ragetti	MACKENZIE CROOK
Davy Jones	BILL NIGHY

Audio Story Produced by RANDY THORNTON
and TED KRYCZKO
Engineered and co-produced by JEFF SHERIDAN
Adapted by BARBARA BAZULDUA
℗WALT DISNEY RECORDS

Printed in Malaysia
First Edition
1 3 5 7 9 10 8 6 4 2
Library of Congress Catalog Card Number: 2007903439
ISBN-13: 978-1-4231-0918-1
ISBN-10: 1-4231-0918-X
Visit DISNEYPIRATES.COM

Based on the screenplay written by Ted Elliott & Terry Rossio

Based on characters created by Ted Elliott & Terry Rossio and Stuart Beattie and Jay Wolpert

Based on Walt Disney's Pirates of the Caribbean

Produced by Jerry Bruckheimer

Directed by Gore Verbinski

Disney
PRESS

New York

At the docks in Singapore, a woman's voice rose through the swirling fog. "A call to all, pay heed the squall." Moments later, Elizabeth Swann stepped out of her small boat. Chinese pirates surrounded her instantly. Their leader, Tai Huang glared at her.

"A dangerous song to be singing, for any who are ignorant of its meaning."

Suddenly, Captain Hector Barbossa appeared beside Elizabeth. "Your master's expecting us."

In a crumbling bathhouse, Sao Feng was waiting. He had caught Will Turner trying to steal his ancient navigational charts to the world beyond this one, and he was suspicious. "You intend to attempt a voyage to Davy Jones's Locker. Why?"

Barbossa tossed Sao Feng a silver piece of eight. "We must convene the Brethren Court." The East India Trading Company led by Lord Cutler Beckett was challenging the pirates' rule of the seas. The Brethren had to fight or lose their way of life forever. But one Pirate Lord was missing. "Jack Sparrow holds one of the nine Pieces of Eight. So we must go and get him back."

V ☸ ⛵

Suddenly, the bathhouse windows shattered. East India Trading Company agents poured in, pistols blazing. Explosions rocked the bathhouse. As Elizabeth and Barbossa battled their way back to the dock, Will offered Sao Feng a secret deal in exchange for the charts. Hiding in the shadows, an agent named Mercer heard them. He rushed to tell Beckett what he had learned. The Brethren were convening. But he didn't know where.

For days, Barbossa and his crew sailed through silent, frozen seas. Will studied the ancient charts, rotating the circles and trying to decipher the strange words. "Over the edge, over again, sunrise sets, flash of green."

One of the crew, named Pintel, explained the flash of green. "It signals when a soul comes back to this world from the dead."

In the distance, Will saw white mist, stretching to infinity. Raging water thundered and roared as it pulled the ship over an endless waterfall and into darkness. They had reached the edge of the world.

Barbossa's crew stumbled from their wrecked ship onto a deserted shore. A white hot sun burned in a cloudless sky.

Elizabeth gazed at the endless emptiness. "I don't see Jack."

But Tia Dalma had read the signs. "Witty Jack is closer than you think."

Just then, the *Black Pearl* appeared sailing across the burning desert sands on the backs of ten thousand crabs. Jack Sparrow was at the helm.

Elizabeth ran to greet him. "We've come to rescue you!"

"That's very kind of you. But it would seem that as I possess a ship and you don't, you're the ones in need of rescuing."

But no one knew how to return to the land of the living. If they didn't escape before sunset, they were doomed to sail between the worlds forever.

Jack studied the chart's mysterious words. "Up is down." Suddenly, he understood. They had to roll the boat over. Jack and the crew raced from one side of the ship to the other, rocking it wildly. As the sun began to sink Jack shouted, "And now up . . . is down!"

The *Black Pearl* rolled over and spun back up. A green light flashed on the horizon. They were back.

V ✦ ⚓ ⛵

As the *Pearl* stopped at a small island to fill the water barrels, Sao Feng's ship appeared. And right behind was Beckett on the *Endeavour*. Will had promised to deliver Jack in exchange for command of the *Pearl*. "I need the *Pearl*. That's the only reason I came on this voyage."

Jack was escorted to meet Beckett. He wanted information. "Who are the Pirate Lords? Where are they meeting?" If Jack refused to tell, he would hang.

At last, Jack agreed to lead Beckett to Shipwreck Cove. But being tricky Jack Sparrow, he had his own plans.

V ✹ ⚓

Meanwhile, Barbossa tried to convince Sao Feng to help them escape. Sao Feng thought the odds were too great against them. "They have the *Dutchman*. Now the *Pearl*. And what do the Brethren have?"

"Calypso. The goddess herself, bound in human form."

Sao Feng agreed on one condition. Elizabeth would come with him.

Driving Beckett's men from the *Pearl*, Sao Feng sailed away on the *Empress* under cover of cannon fire from the *Pearl*. Jack flipped a cannon over, tied a rope to its base, and swung back to the *Black Pearl*. Tossing Will in the brig, Jack set sail with the *Endeavour* and *Flying Dutchman* in pursuit.

That night, Sao Feng visited Elizabeth in his luxurious cabin. He believed she was Calypso. Before Elizabeth could explain, explosions, cannon fire, and pistol shot ripped through the night. The *Flying Dutchman* was attacking.

Sao Feng fell with a spear of broken wood buried in his chest. He ripped the Captain's Knot pendant from his chest and gave it to Elizabeth. "Take it. You will be free. Go in my place to Shipwreck Cove, Calypso."

Now Elizabeth was captain of the *Empress* and one of the
Pirate Lords.

But a few moments later, she was a hostage imprisoned in the
Flying Dutchman's brig. She called for Will's father, "Bootstrap."

Slowly, Will's father, "Bootstrap Bill" Turner, emerged from
the ship's hull and warned her about Will's plans to save him. "If
he saves me . . . he loses you. Tell him to stay away. Tell him it's
too late. I'm already a part of the ship."

Later that night, Elizabeth escaped the brig and crawled across the towline back to the *Empress*.

Meanwhile, Will had escaped the *Black Pearl's* brig and was leaving a trail for Beckett. Will wanted to save his father from Davy Jones, but if he succeeded, he knew he would lose Elizabeth. To Will's surprise, Jack offered to stab Jones's heart and bind himself to the *Dutchman*. He gave Will his Compass and shoved him overboard. "My regards to Davy Jones."

When Beckett and Jones plucked Will from the sea, he presented his demands. "You will free my father. And you will guarantee Elizabeth's safety, along with my own." Then he held up Jack's Compass. "What is it you want most?"

The circles of double-crossing deals, betrayals, and secret plans were drawing tighter. And at their center was Shipwreck Cove. As the rocky cliffs of Shipwreck Island came into view, Tia Dalma commanded Barbossa to force the Brethren to free her. Barbossa refused. "It took nine Pirate Lords to bind you, Calypso, and it'll take no less than nine to set you free." He threw her in the brig and sailed into an enormous dark tunnel hidden in the cliffs.

Deep in the island, the Brethren were gathered for the first time in many lifetimes. Barbossa called them to order. "I convene this, the fourth Brethren Court. Your Pieces of Eight, my fellow captains."

One by one, the Pirate Lords tossed their Pieces of Eight into a wooden bowl. But Jack fingered the circlet coin in his braid and hesitated. "Might I point out that we are still short one Pirate Lord, and I'm as content as a cucumber to wait until Sao Feng joins us."

Elizabeth's voice rang out and she strode into the room. "Sao Feng is dead."

Jack was stunned and a little upset to see her wearing the Captain's Knot pendant. "He made you captain?"

But she had even more news: "Our location has been
betrayed. Jones is under the command of Lord Beckett—
they're on their way here." Elizabeth wanted to fight, but the
Pirate Lords believed they had no chance against the *Flying
Dutchman*.

Then Barbossa revealed his plan. "Gentlemen, ladies . . .
we must free Calypso." The pirates roared with anger. The
gathering quickly disintegrated into a pushing, shoving, yelling,
kicking brawl.

Jack agreed with Elizabeth. "We must fight." But according to the Pirate Code, an act of war could only be declared by a Pirate King. And that meant electing one. Every captain voted for themselves. But with both Jack's vote and her own, Elizabeth was elected king of the Brethren. Her orders were simple. "At dawn, we're at war."

Amidst the cheers and shouts, Jack saw Ragetti take the bowl with the Pieces of Eight. But he kept quiet. The pieces of his own plan were now in place.

At dawn, the *Black Pearl* and the pirate fleet prepared for battle. As the *Endeavour* sailed into view through the morning fog, the pirates screamed their bloodcurdling battle cries.

Then the fog lifted, and silence fell. Hundreds of ships— the entire armada of the East India Trading Company— surrounded them. The *Flying Dutchman* was in the lead. All eyes turned to Jack, but he had only one suggestion. "Parlay?"

Meeting on a narrow, windy beach, Elizabeth proposed an exchange. "Will leaves with us, and you can take Jack." As Jack walked toward Beckett, he dropped his circlet coin in the sand. His eyes met Barbossa's.

Beckett was certain of victory. He didn't see Barbossa pick up the coin and close his fist around it. Barbossa had Jack Sparrow's Piece of Eight. And now he was going to do what he had always wanted—release Calypso.

Back on the *Pearl*, Ragetti tied Tia Dalma to the mast and bound her hands. Barbossa tore the Captain's Knot from Elizabeth's throat, dropped it in the bowl, and set the Pieces on fire. Then Ragetti spoke: "Calypso, I release you from your human bonds."

Tia Dalma began to grow. The ropes and manacles snapped as she rose, towering above them. Barbossa knelt before her. "Unleash your fury upon those who dare pretend themselves your masters . . . or mine."

Calypso screamed! Then she dissolved onto the deck in the form of ten thousand crabs. They scurried over the side of the ship. She was gone. And so were Barbossa's hopes.

There was only one choice left. Fight. Elizabeth sounded the call. "Listen! The Brethren will still be looking to the *Black Pearl* to lead. Gentlemen . . . hoist the colors." On every ship, the pirates' fleet echoed her cry and raised their flags. The ships surged forward, and the wind began to rise. Clouds swirled overhead, forming a whirling disk of blackness. Lightning stabbed the sea and where it hit, a giant whirlpool opened. The *Black Pearl* and *Flying Dutchman* plunged into the swirling abyss.

The two ships spun closer, their giant masts tilting toward
each other. Jones's crew swarmed onto the *Black Pearl*.
Fighting beside Elizabeth, Will shouted over the din.
"Elizabeth, will you marry me? I love you!"

Elizabeth parried an attacker and shouted to Barbossa,
"Marry us!" Barbossa raced through the ceremony. There was
time for one kiss—and the fight was on again.

On the *Dutchman*, Jack grabbed the chest from Jones's cabin and swung up into the rigging. Jones was right behind. The key to the chest was clutched in one of his tentacles.

Jack slashed that tentacle off. It fell, writhing and spurting black ink. As the ships' masts slammed together, Jack dropped the chest and fell. Jones caught it and heaved Jack into the air. But Jack grabbed a line, swung down and snatched a pistol from a crewman. "My pistol!"

Will swung over from the *Black Pearl*, grabbed the chest, and ran. But Bootstrap Bill stood in his way. Not recognizing him, he slashed at Will furiously. "It's me! It's Will, your son." As Will defended himself, the chest slid from his grasp.

V ☸ ⛵

Elizabeth swung to the *Dutchman* and held Jones at bay as Jack crawled to the chest clutching the key. Will rushed to defend her, but with an evil grin Jones plunged his sword into Will. As Will lay dying in Elizabeth's arms, Jack knew what had to be done. He buried his sword in Jones's heart. But Will's hand was on the hilt. With an unearthly scream, Jones clutched his chest and plummeted into the abyss. Will Turner was the *Dutchman*'s new captain.

But the *Dutchman* was dragging the *Black Pearl* into the abyss. Firing cannons, Barbossa blasted the tangled masts apart. Holding Elizabeth, Jack swung off the *Dutchman* as it vanished beneath the waves.

But the *Endeavour* was bearing down, preparing to blast the *Pearl* into oblivion. Suddenly, the *Flying Dutchman* soared from the depths. Will Turner was in command. His eyes blazed with avenging anger. Trapping the *Endeavour* between them, Will and Barbossa blew Beckett and his ship away. The battle was won.

As pirate cheers rang out, Will freed his father. But Bootstrap refused to leave his son.

V ☸ ⛵

On a deserted beach, Elizabeth met Will one last time. She promised to keep the chest safe for his return. Then he was gone.

Ten years passed. One sunset, Elizabeth sat on the beach with her son and a familiar chest. As she watched the horizon, a flash of green lit her face. Will was coming home.